SNOWY TRAILS

A Collection of
SHORT STORIES

Jan-Carol
Publishing, Inc

"every story needs a book"

Snowy Trails
A Collection of Short Stories

Published September 2019
Mountain Girl Press
Imprint of Jan-Carol Publishing, Inc
Copyright © 2019

ISBN: 9781950895199
Library of Congress Control Number: 2019950381

You may contact the publisher:
Jan-Carol Publishing, Inc.
PO Box 701
Johnson City, TN 37605
publisher@jancarolpublishing.com
jancarolpublishing.com

This is dedicated to all the talented authors for their participation in this collection of short stories, and to all the readers of Jan-Carol Publishing's books.

TABLE OF CONTENTS

A Birthday Party

Jan Howery

Yup! The storm'll set in before noon today," Pa said as he stepped out of his farmhouse onto the front porch. "I'd better get that Christmas tree! If I don't, we may not have a tree, or I'll be trying to drag it through six feet of snow."

"Ah, Pa. You are just as excited as the grandchildren!" Ma answered as she followed him to the front door. "Are you sure about the storm?"

Pa walked back inside and answered, "Yup. You can smell bad weather in the air, and the clouds don't lie."

The mood was interrupted when six-year-old Martha Jane asked, "Will Daddy be home for Christmas?"

The Civil War had been over for four years. Martha Jane's dad, Ma's son, had joined the army in 1864 before he had known that his wife was pregnant with a son. Ma's son James was only 26 when he marched with the rebels, fighting for something that wasn't part of their lives. His wife, Rosemary, was young and beautiful and had made a blushing bride at the age of 16. But now she was a widower with two small children. She couldn't manage on her own, so she had moved in with her in-laws on the day that James had gone to fight in a brother-against-brother war.

The government never made a formal notice, but after the war ended and Ma and Pa never heard whether James was dead or alive, they had to assume that he had been killed. They wanted to believe that he had been taken as a prisoner and shipped out west, that he maybe hadn't survived the trip. It was better than believing that he was brutally killed and left dying on a horrifying,

1

bloody battlefield.

Rosemary walked to the hallway when Martha Jane asked the question about her daddy. Ma and Rosemary exchanged looks, and Ma answered, "Martha Jane, we had this talk. Do you remember? I told you that your Daddy was in heaven and that he celebrates Jesus's birthday on Christmas with Jesus. It's a big birthday party."

"Why can't they come to our house? We can have a birthday party here for Jesus!" Martha Jane asked so innocently.

"Because our house isn't large enough," Rosemary quickly answered. "Now, go and check on Jim."

Ma and Rosemary exchanged a smile as Martha Jane ran down the hallway and headed upstairs to check on her brother. "Is Pa going out to get a tree?" Rosemary asked. "I can't believe that it's already Christmas Eve."

"Yes. He'd better hurry. He thinks that this storm's going to be a big one," Ma replied.

"Yup. You wait and see. Mark my words. This storm'll be a big one. We're definitely going to have a white Christmas," Pa stated as he put on his boots and heavy coat. "Ma, I will be back in a couple of hours. I should be back by dinner time."

"Be careful, Pa," Ma yelled to Pa as he went out the back door.

"I think that I already see some snowflakes falling," Rosemary stated. "It's already starting to snow. Look!"

Ma walked to the window so she could watch the snow gently start to fall. She looked out the window and wished that she could see her son James walk up the hillside to come home. Each Christmas it seemed harder for her to accept that James would not be coming home. Christmas time was a special time for the family, and James had loved everything about Christmas.

Ma's son Henry, James's old brother, and his family lived about half of a mile away from the home place. Henry had bought a large farm that connected to Ma and Pa's property. Henry, his wife, and their two sons and two daughters would be joining the family on Christmas Eve and staying over for Santa Claus's visit. It was a family tradition that had continued even with James's absence.

"Oh my! Look, Rosemary. That snow is starting to stick. I think that Pa is right. We're in for a big snow—a white Christmas for sure," Ma said.

Rosemary peeked out the window and said, "Oh yes. Looks like it." She paused and then excused herself to go upstairs and check on her children. She missed James, and her sadness was not easy to hide, especially during Christmas. James had loved Christmas, and Rosemary missed him and the kid-like excitement he had during the holiday.

Time passed quickly, but Pa did not return in a couple of hours.

"He should have been home by now," Ma said. "He said that he would be here for dinner, and here it is after two p.m. I'm worried. He's been gone for several hours. It's not like him to miss dinner time. We'll soon be getting ready for supper. You know...I think that I'll go look for him."

"Ma, maybe he just got to talking to someone. You know Pa. He likes people," Rosemary said. "Surely he'll be back soon. Let's get the decorations from the attic and see what we can put on the tree when he gets here."

"Well, I guess," Ma answered. "But look at the snow, Rosemary. It's really coming down, and there must be at least six inches of snow already."

"Try not to worry, Ma. We need to get to baking and cooking. Don't you think? The children are taking their afternoon naps, and now is a good time to get to cooking," Rosemary said, trying to distract Ma.

"You go ahead and get started in the kitchen. I've got to go get help. There's something wrong. Pa should have been back hours ago."

"You can't go out looking for Pa," Rosemary said. "Henry and his family should be here soon."

"I'm worried. I'll walk to Henry's and get him, and maybe he'll go with me to look for Pa," Ma said.

"I'm worried too," Rosemary said, tears gleaming in her eyes.

"We've got to do something. The snow is not letting up, and he could've fallen or gotten lost. But we have to do something," Ma said.

"I'll go with you," Rosemary said.

"No. You need to stay here with the children and start the cooking," Ma answered. "I will take the lantern, and I'll be fine to walk to Henry's. And Henry may be on his way here anyway."

Both women became very quiet as Ma dressed for the snowy outdoors. As she pulled on her boots and started down the hallway to the front door, there was a loud knock at the front door. It was so loud that it startled both Rosemary and Ma.

Ma, who was catching her breath, exclaimed, "Oh, thank God! That must be Pa." She ran to the door, and when she opened it, she gasped. "What?!"

Standing on the front porch was a young man covered with snow, and he was holding Pa over his shoulder. As he sat Pa down on the porch, it became clear that the young man was wearing an old, battered confederate jacket.

"Ma'am, I think that he fell, and when I found him, he was unconscious," the young man said.

"Pa!" Ma yelled. "Bring him inside. Is he hurt?"

Pa groaned as he was helped inside. He was coming around and was trying to speak. "I fell...I fell down."

"It's alright, Pa. You're soaked," Ma said. "Rosemary, heat up some water, get some hot coffee, and get him some dry clothes. Young man, help me get him to the sitting room so he can be near the fireplace."

The young man carried Pa into the sitting room and sat him down in a chair, and Ma started removing Pa's wet clothes. Pa was trying to speak, but he was chilled to the bone. "Pa, don't try to speak. You're okay. This young man helped you," Ma said. "Thank you, young man. What is your name?"

The young man never answered. Ma didn't really pay any attention as she continued to remove Pa's wet clothing. Rosemary entered the sitting room carrying hot coffee and clean clothes. When Ma looked up, she asked, "Where is the young man? Where did he go?"

"I'm not sure," Rosemary answered. "He was here."

Rosemary walked back to the front door. The young man was standing there with the Christmas tree that Pa had cut. "Ma'am, would you like for me to bring this inside for you?" he asked.

Rosemary stared at him. He was probably the same age as her James, and he had the same height, build, and sky blue eyes. For a moment Rosemary saw her James.

"Ma'am, would you like the tree in the sitting room?" the young man asked again.

Rosemary stuttered, "Oh yes. That would be perfect. And you must be freezing. I will get you a cup of coffee and some dry clothes." Rosemary was starting to close the door when she heard a voice.

"Hey, don't shut that door. We don't want to spend the night in this snowstorm," Henry yelled.

Henry and his family had arrived in their horse drawn sleigh. "What a white Christmas!"

"Henry, come on in. Pa's been hurt. He fell and had to be carried home,"

Rosemary announced.

"You and the kids should go on inside, and I will put the horses in the barn," Henry directed.

Rosemary and Henry's wife and kids walked into the sitting room. The glow of the fire highlighted the young man's features as he set up the Christmas tree. "I hope that this is okay," he said.

"Oh yes!" Rosemary said. "Here is a cup of coffee, and I found these clothes. I think that they will fit you. They...well...you can go into the side bedroom and change." The clothes had belonged to James. Rosemary felt a sense of sadness, but at the same time, a feeling of joy came over her.

"Well, look at this tree," Pa whispered. "Let's get to decorating it. I knew it would be perfect."

"Pa, take it easy," Ma said.

"I'm fine, thanks to this young man," Pa said.

The young man stood next to the tree and seemed to glow with a halo from the fireplace. "I must be going," he said.

"What? Absolutely not," Ma said. "You can't go back out in that storm. Can't you stay with us? Where is your family? Can't be near. Can't you stay and help us celebrate Christmas? Having Pa back here all in one piece is a Christmas gift, and you're a Christmas blessing! If it hadn't been for you..." Ma's words faded into a thoughtful sadness.

"Well, if you don't mind, I guess I am sort of snowed in," the young man responded.

"Take off your jacket and put on those dry clothes. I hope your family won't be worried, but you are staying here tonight," Ma said. "We have plenty of room for you, and you are more than welcome. Now, go put on those dry clothes."

The young man removed his jacket and placed it over a rocking chair next to the Christmas tree. He left and quickly returned wearing James's clothes. The clothes fit perfectly.

"What is your name?" Rosemary asked.

"Just call me 'J,'" the young man answered. He smiled at Rosemary, and she found his smile engaging.

"'J?' That must stand for something," Rosemary stated. But the young man ignored her comment.

It was Christmas Eve, so Rosemary brought in the decorations, and the family ate food, sang Christmas carols, and decorated the Christmas tree. They laughed, told stories, and put the kids to bed so they could wait for Santa Claus to leave presents under the tree. Rosemary noticed that 'J' seemed comfortable while getting the kids to go to sleep and that the children took to him very quickly.

"This has been one of the best Christmas Eves we've had in such a long time," Ma said.

"Yes, and you, young man...you made this happen. Thank you," Pa said.

"Believe me...you've made this the best Christmas that I've had in a long time too," the young man replied.

The snow continued to fall all night. By morning there was more than a foot of snow. Rosemary and Ma were the first to get up, and they started cooking breakfast.

Ma went from room to room and instructed, "Get up! Breakfast time! Santa Claus may have left a present or two under the tree for you."

The kids were excited and started running around while everyone else slowly made their way to the kitchen table, except for the young man. "I guess he's not used to having a home-cooked breakfast. Rosemary, why don't you go get him?" Ma instructed.

Rosemary walked to the side bedroom and knocked on the door. "Breakfast is ready." When no one answered, Rosemary slowly opened the door. The room was empty, and the bed had not been slept in.

Rosemary ran back to the kitchen. "Ma, he's not there. The bed hasn't been slept in."

Pa walked in from the sitting room carrying the young man's confederate jacket. His face was white and pale, and there was a blankness in his stare. He was carrying the jacket in one hand and a note in the other. Ma and Rosemary stared at the jacket, and Ma took the note from Pa's hand. She read the note out loud:

"Best Christmas in four years. I am sorry that I didn't get a chance to say goodbye, but I had a very important Birthday Party Celebration to attend. Merry Christmas!"

Appalachian Christmas Eve Storm

Betty Kossick

Twelve-year-old Billy Ray draws back the yellow-ruffled curtain of his momma's kitchen window. He thinks he hears voices outside. "It's a mean storm out there," he says aloud, then wonders, *who would be traipsin' in the blindin' snow on such a night, 'specially on Christmas Eve.*

Suzanna, his momma, calls to him, "What's up, Billy Ray?"

"I think someone's outside, Momma; I do." Billy Ray answers while continuing to peer out the window. "Sure enough, it's those city folks whose kids are new at Stewart School. I've seen the momma pickin' up her daughter, Rachel, and her son, Robert, at school. Rachel's in my class. Her brother's in eighth grade. Rachel says they moved here from Nashville a few weeks ago. They's all a'carryin' big pokes with them. The mister's carryin' two, and so's the missus."

"Oh yes," Suzanna says. "I met the momma and the pa when I carried over a 'welcome loaf.' The young'uns were in school. But why's they comin' out in this storm...on Christmas Eve? They surely aren't comin' a'carolin'. I don't hear any singin'."

"Pa, we're gettin' company!" Billy Ray calls out as he rushes to the door to greet the unlikely stormy-night guests. Opening the door proves to be a big task. The wind blows so hard against the lad that he almost falls backwards. By this time Billy Ray's parents; his teenage brother, Jesse; his six-year-old sister, Belinda; and their dog, Charlie, are gathered in the hallway. All of them are wondering the same thing as Billy Ray: *What's up?*

"It looks like the neighbors are comin' bearin' food parcels from the Food Fair Market. Can't miss those red, striped, paper pokes they has at Christmas time," David, Billy's pa, announces, a blush on his face and his brow furrowed.

The Bradley family members smile happily as they rush through the door and stomp their feet free of snow. Billy Ray tries to hold the door steady against the forceful wind, and fifteen-year-old Jesse runs to his aid and forces the door closed. Fortunately, a long, well-crafted oak bench sits right beside the door, and the Bradley's all set down their loads on the floor while taking off their boots. They shout, "Merry Christmas!"

"Merry Christmas to you too, but what's this all about?" David inquires.

"Well..." Mr. Bradley starts explaining as he and his family pick up their grocery bags and walk directly into the kitchen, setting the bags down on the kitchen table. The Dawson family follows them. "We're the Bradley's, and we haven't been living here long, but we heard that you lost your job and that your wife has been through a couple of years fighting cancer, so it doesn't take a lot of figuring to know that it takes a heap of money to feed four mouths. Five, actually, because we know there's a dog in your family. He trotted along with Suzanna to our house on the day she came with her delicious loaf of 'welcome bread.'"

He continues, "Our church in town asked its members if we knew anyone who might be in need of a Christmas hug in the way of groceries. I'm sorry that we haven't come to meet you folks sooner, but getting settled in with our work and setting up the house have been so time-consuming that we've been flopping into bed every night. But we figured that Christmas Eve would be a good time to say hello, so we mentioned to our church that your family might be feeling a tight crunch financially, that you are close-by neighbors, and that we'd be happy to do the shopping and bring it to you on Christmas Eve."

"Wait, neighbor, I 'preciate your good thoughts, but we aren't a charity case," David blurts out, his flushed face turning redder as he speaks.

Suzanna draws herself closer to David and straightens herself by his shoulder, which makes her appear taller. "My David doesn't mean you no offense. We's just never been needin' before this."

She continues, "David, it's my fault. When I took the bread loaf to their house after they moved in, I mentioned to Mrs. Bradley...Peggy...that I felt poorly about it being such a little loaf. I always prefer to make generous ones, but I mentioned that you'd been out of work for a few months, that I was rationin' my flour, and that I'd be bringin' another mightier loaf when you gets to workin' good again. I'm sorry, honey."

David draws his wife closer to his side, "It's okay, Suzanna. You meant well—"

"Pa, look," Belinda exclaims, interrupting him. "Look what's in the one poke—it's a big poke of Buddy's Dog Food. Can we keep that for Charlie? Please, Pa?"

"Excuse me, Mr. Dawson. We don't want you to think of this as charity. It's a Christmas gift," Mr. Bradley implores. "Our little church prayed for the right folks to help this Christmas time. There are others who are being helped with these Christmas hugs too. There are many families hurting during the down economy. We've heard that you've been working hard, doing all kinds of odd jobs, and using your fine carpenter skills. And we also know that you can't be making a bunch of money either, since employment isn't plentiful to find right now. We'd be obliged if you'd accept this as a friendship gift. Actually, it was our Rachel who reminded us on the way to the store not to forget food for Charlie. She urged us to get right to the pet food aisle first. And Robert picked out a chew-bone for Charlie too."

Breaking into a broad smile, David grasps his new neighbor's shoulder. "It sounds like Charlie's made a hit with you Bradley folks. I'll make you a bargain. If the church will allow us to be payin' for it after I gets work again—to help someone else when they're needin'—we'll say thank you for your mighty large thoughtfulness."

"It's a good bargain," Mr. Bradley smiles.

"No, it ain't unless we's on first name callin'." Extending his hand, he says, "My name's David. What's yours?"

"It happens to be the same as your pooch. I'm Charlie," he answers as he clasps his new friend's strong hand.

"Charlie's a fine name," David acknowledges as he watches Charlie reach down to pet the dog named Charlie, who had been leaning against Charlie's pant leg.

"Please, pick a seat, all of you. Sit down and rest yourself from fightin' that hard wind to get in here," David says. "I need to apologize for not gettin' over to meet you too. I've been drivin' to the next county to get work, leavin' mighty early and gettin' back mighty late. The mountain's been growin' with new folks movin' in. When Suzanna and me first married, this was just a speck of a town up here. In sixteen years, Stewartville's changed a whole lot. We feel it's a mighty fine place to rear-up young'uns. You won't be regrettin' movin' here."

"There wasn't any such thing as the Pink Ribbon Winners back when we set up housekeepin'. Since you're aware of my Suzanna's experience with cancer, I suppose you must also have heard about how she's organized the Stewartville community to raise funds for breast cancer awareness. She did it all while fightin' her own battle. But she's doin' just fine now." David says.

"Yes, I'm mighty grateful for God's mercy," Suzanna says as she excuses herself from the group.

David continues, "Me and the kids are mighty proud of her for inventin' the Pink Ribbon Winner marches, but we're even prouder of her for her own fightin' spirit and for overcomin' the disease. Now she's organizin' 'The Victors' for the menfolk who have breast cancer. Can you believe that we men can get breast cancer too? Never knew it until my sweet one got into the fray. Now she visits other women in the hospital, helping them adjust and learn all they need to know about breast cancer. Belinda goes visitin' with her momma sometimes too. My Suzanna knows how to involve people in doin' the right good things in life. Stewartville sorta thinks of her as its hometown hero. In fact, the *Stewartville Clarion* newspaper calls her just that in a story they published. I can't help but brag on her because she's a good woman who's got what's called an in-dom-it-able spirit."

Charlie chimes in, "I think you can count on four more helpers right here with us too. Peggy and I will be glad to get involved. Volunteerism is a good thing to do. Our kids, Robert and Rachel, have been volunteers for one thing or another since they've been in school. They both enjoy helping worthy causes. I'm also wondering, David, if you might consider letting us hire you to do some work for us? We need bookcases built in our living room, and we need a laundry room, or mud room, built off the kitchen."

"Charlie, I think that Suzanna can arrange the volunteer offer, and I'm available any time you need for the carpentry work." David grins, then adds, "I've been doin' lots of odd jobs these past few months, but carpentry is my specialty. My poppa was before me, and my grandpoppa was before him. That's in our blood."

Suzanna calls out from the kitchen, "I've just made a pot of warm choclit' to warm y'all up. Come and git it." Belinda claps, and Charlie, the dog, barks excitedly as Jesse opens the poke of Buddy's dog food for him. Robert pulls over Charlie's bowl to fill it with the food.

"But, Momma," Billy Ray notes, "we don't have any peppermint sticks for stirrin' and meltin' in the chocolit'. It's not Christmas Eve without that smell and taste."

"Oh yes, you do," Robert points out. "There is a whole box of candy canes somewhere among those groceries."

David's eyes brighten as he says, "You folks thought of everythin'. Bless you."

After Suzanna fills all the mugs, David uses his candy cane to stir the chocolate within his cup, then lifts his mug to make a toast to the Bradley's. "Merry Christmas! New neighbors is a mighty fine Christmas gift."

The Best Gift

Cheryl Livingston

The snow crunched under the delicate heels of Muffy's boots as she and her father strolled through the city park. "Oh, Daddy," she exclaimed, "I love taking walks in the snow!" Privately, she thought, "Especially when I can guide him over to the stores!"

Wilson responded fondly, "Yes, dear, the Christmas decorations are rather attractive, don't you think?"

Muffy turned up her dainty little nose and sniffed, "They are a little tacky, but I suppose they will do." Pulling on her father's arm, she ran to a store window. "Daddy! Just look at this pearl ring! Isn't it simply marvelous?"

"Lovely, but it's a little too mature for my baby girl," Wilson responded.

She whined, "No, it's not. Daddy, I really must have that ring for Christmas!"

"Muffy, dear, I really don't think that is a wise choice for a girl your age," Wilson said.

"But, Daddy, I waaant it!" Muffy cried.

"Muffy, you know I would do anything for you, but that ring is very expensive. What if you lose it?" asked Wilson.

Batting her eyelashes at him, she said, "But I won't lose it, Daddy..."

After a moment of thought, Wilson said resolutely, "No, Muffy, it isn't a good choice. Let's look at something more fitting for your age."

Stamping her foot, Muffy howled, "I want it! I want it! I want it!"

Furtively glancing around, Wilson said quietly, "Muffy, don't cause a scene here in the middle of town! Someone might see us!"

Pouting, Muffy exclaimed, "I don't care! If I can't have that ring, I'll hold my breath till I turn blue." In an increasingly melodramatic voice, she wailed, "Yes, I'll hold my breath until I faint dead away, right here on the street, and then everyone will gather around and start talking about us! Then they'll call the doctor, and he will ask what happened, and you will have to tell him that I fainted from a broken heart! Then what will the neighbors say?"

As she gave him a sly glance from the side of her eye, Wilson grabbed her arm and guided her into the store. "All right, all right. You can have the ring. Just be a good girl and be quiet!"

❋ ❋ ❋

Wilson glanced up from his newspaper as his servant began filling his plate with a selection of eggs and bacon. Beatrice, Muffy's mother, was admiring her reflection in a small silver mirror as Muffy held out her hand toward her. "Mother, did you see the ring Daddy bought me for Christmas yesterday? I saw it downtown and simply had to have it!"

Beatrice exclaimed, "It is stunning—just right for a girl your age!" At this statement Wilson looked up in surprise, shook his head in disbelief, and then ducked behind his paper again.

"Daddy thought it was too old for me," Muffy said petulantly.

"My goodness, Wilson, she isn't a baby anymore. She just takes after her mother. We both love the finer things in life, don't we, dear?" she said, patting Muffy's hand.

Resigned, Wilson said, "Yes, I'm well aware of your penchant for expensive trinkets, Beatrice. And that brings me to something I need to talk about. It seems that in order to keep making the money to support this family, I must go on an extended business trip. I'll be leaving next week."

"But Christmas is just two weeks away," Beatrice protested. "How long will you be gone?"

Wilson replied, "I should be back by the end of January. Muffy will have to return to school before I get back, but there's no reason that you can't go with me, Beatrice."

Thrilled at the thought of an adventure, Beatrice bustled out of the room and started talking to herself. "New restaurants to dine in! New stores to explore! I must go tell the maid what to pack!"

Stricken, Muffy said plaintively, "But what about me?"

"I've already checked with your Aunt Sara and Uncle Joe. They said they would love to have you stay with them for the holidays."

Incredulous, Muffy said, "Aunt Sara and Uncle Joe? Please tell me you are joking!"

"Joking? I don't think so. Sara is my sister, and she loves you dearly. Besides, your cousins are close to your age. I don't see any reason why you shouldn't go," Wilson said dismissively.

"But, Daddy...they're poor!"

❄ ❄ ❄

Sara put her arm around the stiff young girl and said, "We're just so glad you could come to see us, Muffy! Emma and Billy are real excited to see you again after all these years! Families shouldn't stay away from each other for so long! Billy, Emma, here's your long lost cousin."

A freckled-faced girl who appeared to be about seven years old jumped up from the old sofa. "Hi! I'm glad you're here. We're going to have lots of fun!"

The older brother shuffled forward shyly. "Yeah, me too."

Muffy stood silently and eyed Emma's faded dress and the holes in Billy's shoes. As she stared around the room, she noticed that her uncle Joe's hands were red and chapped and that her aunt Sara's hair was in a simple knot at the back of her neck. The room was furnished with chipped chairs and a threadbare rug. The more she saw, the more uncomfortable she became. With a pang of homesickness, she missed her own beautiful home. Then Emma broke the stifling silence by grabbing Muffy's hand. "Come on. I'll show you where you're going to be sleeping!"

❄ ❄ ❄

Emma announced with a flourish, "Well, here we are! You can hang your clothes over there. I usually sleep on the right side of the bed, but you can have it if you want."

"The right side? Do you mean that we must share a bed?" Muffy asked incredulously as she took in the homemade quilt that covered the rather lumpy looking mattress. Then in a quieter tone she continued, "I can't believe Daddy sent me here."

"You mean you didn't want to come?" Emma asked sympathetically. "I'm so sorry, but we really will have fun! Christmas is a great time of year. There's always so much to do!"

"Like what?" Muffy asked hopefully. Visions of dancing with a tall, young stranger under the mistletoe started darting through her mind.

"Well, we can help Mom with the cooking and baking. I just love to make the gingerbread! We go caroling, and there's always a really good service at church," Emma said with her never-ending enthusiasm.

Muffy said, "But what about the shopping, the dining out, and the parties?"

"We make most of our gifts for each other, and there aren't too many places around here to dine out. And parties? Well, after caroling we all get together and drink hot chocolate and eat cookies!" Emma said.

With a sarcastic edge to her voice, Muffy said, "Oh goodie! I can hardly wait."

Muffy and Emma both looked toward the door as Billy entered. "Well, are ya settled in yet? Wow! You really have a lot of luggage. Why did you bring so much? You can only wear one dress at a time, ya know?"

"My, aren't you the critic? I'll have you know that I was voted 'Best Dressed' at my school this year!" Muffy replied haughtily.

Emma reached out, gently and wistfully stroking one of Muffy's hats. "That sure is a pretty bonnet. I wish I had one, but they're too expensive."

Muffy replied, "I have five of them in different colors. I suppose you could wear one of them while I'm here."

With an exasperated eye roll, Billy exclaimed, "Let's quit all this gabbing and go do something! Hey, Muffy, ya wanna go feed the pigs?"

Becoming resigned to her fate of a holiday spent in the country, Muffy replied, "By all means, just show me the way."

❅ ❅ ❅

Stumbling back into the house, laughing and breathless, Billy hooted, "Muffy, you looked really funny when you slipped. I thought I was gonna bust a gut from laughing when I saw you out there wallowing like a hog!"

"Ha! Ha! Well, you looked also pretty funny when you tried to help me up and then fell! You looked as though you were doing the foxtrot!" Muffy giggled while wiping the mud off her nose.

Eyes wide with curiosity, Emma asked, "Foxtrot? What's a foxtrot?"

Raising her nose in the air, Muffy replied, "Oh, how backwater! I forgot you all just got electricity last month."

Giving her arm a gentle shove, Billy said, "Now, don't you go getting on that fancy high horse of yours. You were having fun just a minute ago." Billy grabbed her arm and began tickling her. "Come on. Admit it! You were having fun! Admit it! Admit it!"

Giggling, Muffy gasped, "All right, all right. I admit it. I was having fun." She caught her breath and asked, "So, what do we do next?"

"I can answer that question," Joe said as he stuck his head into the room. "I'd say you kids better go wash up for supper before Sara tans your hides!"

❋ ❋ ❋

Patting his stomach and leaning back in his chair, Joe groans, "That was a mighty fine meal!" Cocking his head, he continued, "Muffy, that's also some mighty fine music you've got playing there on the Victrola. I'd like to stay and listen, but I've got to go finish up my chores."

As he walked out, Muffy bragged, "I'm getting more recordings for Christmas. I'm also getting a fur muff and a new outfit. And my Daddy bought me this ring! What are you two getting?"

"Oh, that's a beautiful ring, Muffy! I don't know what I'm getting. I've outgrown my petticoats, so maybe that's what I'll get," Emma responded.

Billy added, "I think I'm getting new boots." Holding up his foot so the girls could see, he continued, "These pinch a little."

"That's all? Petticoats and shoes? I'm going to show you how to get what you really want!" Muffy exclaimed.

Dramatically dropping to the couch, she began to cry, "Oh, boo hoo! That's all right, Mother. I don't really have to have that new dress. Of course, I'll be the laughingstock of all my friends. But that's all right." She sniffed delicately. "I can handle their catty remarks." After wiping a tear, her look of utter despair changed to a big smile as she jumped up and said, "There! That is how you get whatever you want!"

Billy and Emma exchanged a look. "I don't think that would work with us, Muffy," Emma said slowly.

"Well, if that doesn't work, you can always throw a tantrum—that's how I got my ring!" Muffy exclaimed as she held up her hand so they could see her ring again.

Billy responded, "Muffy, that wouldn't work for us either, and I'll tell you why. 'Cause Dad would take a hickory switch to our legs—that's why!"

"Corporal punishment?" Muffy asked with amazement. "Why, that's simply unheard of in this day and time."

Emma wriggled in her seat as she asked, "But, Muffy, Christmas is for giving. What are you giving your parents for Christmas?"

With a puzzled look on her face, Muffy replied, "Giving? Well, I haven't even thought about it."

Jumping up, Billy exclaimed, "Boy, I have! I've been whittling a long time on a statue of a bear for Dad and a deer for Mom." Retrieving his figurines, he asked, "Would you like to see? Mom says I have a talent for carving."

Emma excitedly inserted, "And I've been sewing. I made an apron for Mom and some hankies for Dad, and I can't tell you what I made for Billy, 'cause he's standing here!"

Muffy looked at the carvings with amazement. "You made them yourself? They are beautiful. And you're giving them to your parents? You must love them a lot."

A little confused, Emma responded, "Of course we do! But I'm sure you feel the same way about your parents, Muffy."

"Uh...yeah...of course I do," came Muffy's halting reply.

Muffy's discomfort came to a sudden end as Joe and Sara walked in. "Let's go, kids! Time for church!"

❋ ❋ ❋

Stamping the snow off their boots, they filed into an open pew. Leaning over, Muffy whispered to her cousins, "I've never been to church. What's going to happen?"

"NEVER BEEN TO CH—" Billy's loud exclamation was shushed quickly by his mother. Whispering this time, he said, "Never been to church? Where did you grow up...a cave?"

Emma hissed to her brother, "Billy, that's not nice!" Turning to her cousin, she said, "Muffy, it's hard for us to understand because we've been coming to church since we were born." Forgetting to whisper, she continued enthusiastically, "I think you'll like it! There's singing and music, and..." At a stern look from Joe, she continued in a quieter tone, "There's also preaching and praying. But no matter what happens, I always feel God right here beside me."

"God? Right here?" Muffy looked around worriedly. "I don't know if I like that idea. Isn't God some mean, old, scary man who orders people around?"

Forgetting to whisper, Billy responded, "Boy, do you have it all wrong!" This time he sank low in the pew as his mother frowned at him.

With a nudge to Muffy's ribs, Emma breathed, "I think you're going to find out 'cause service is getting ready to start!"

Muffy listened closely as the small choir began a sweet song about a baby being born in a manger. During the second selection Muffy wondered who the three kings were that traveled such a long distance. In the final hymn she learned that angels sang praises of a newborn king. Could this baby they were singing about be God Himself? *Hmm...I've never thought of God as a baby*, she mused with her eyes closed. It was so peaceful that she thought she could almost go to sleep.

"HALLELUJAH!" The sudden loud noise jerked Muffy to attention. Her eyes snapped open to see the pastor standing in the front of the church. "PRAISE THE LORD!" he shouted.

I understood that we were supposed to be quiet in church, Muffy thought, *but he is certainly loud*. Scooting a little closer to Billy, she wasn't sure she was going to like this part of the service. Shrinking down in the pew a little, she quickly glanced around. No one else seemed to be scared, so she decided to focus on the man's words.

As she listened, she was transported to a different place and time. She was in Bethlehem, smelling the straw and feeling the warmth of the animals' bodies. She watched as the shepherds came to pay homage to the new baby king. She gasped as King Herod gave orders to find the baby. Finally, she began to cry as the pastor explained the reason this baby king was born. It seemed too good to be true. Jesus came to take away the sin of the world and to give new life to each person who believed and accepted Him as their Savior.

"This is the Christmas season, and I want you to know that God has a wonderful gift for you," the preacher said. "It is the gift of forgiveness and eternal life, and if you want to accept it, it is yours tonight."

Sara, seeing Muffy's tears, knelt in front of her and asked, "Muffy, are you crying because you believe what the preacher said?" Muffy nodded and said, "I-I-I...I want to receive the gift of Jesus. I want Him to be my Savior!"

❄ ❄ ❄

In a flour-dusted kitchen two heads intently leaned over the counter. With a flourish, Muffy finished icing her stocking-shaped cookie, then breathed, "It's beautiful!" Her smile quickly turned to a grimace as Billy sneaked up behind her and snatched the cookie from her fingers. "Tastes beautiful too!" he laughed, then rubbed his belly.

"Billy!" Emma shouted. "You're as mean as ol' man Greene's turkey!"

"Gobble, gobble, gobble!" Cookie crumbs from the gingerbread boy sprayed from Billy's mouth.

"You're just making a big old mess, Billy!" Emma squealed at her brother.

Looking around at the battered bowls, utensils, and ingredients strewn across the counters and tables, Billy said, "You didn't need my help—you two made a mess without me!"

Infuriated, Emma started toward her brother. He danced out of her reach with a sing-song taunt, "Can't reach me, can't reach me!"

Seeing an argument in the making, Muffy stepped in. "Hey, let's just all pitch in, and then we can go feed the broken cookies to the horse."

Realizing Muffy's suggestion sounded a lot more fun than arguing, Emma picked up a dishrag and began wiping the counter. Before long the girls were singing, and Billy was keeping time by two-stepping with the broom.

✳ ✳ ✳

Joe put down his book and turned to Sara. "Well, tomorrow is Christmas!"

Putting down her mending, Sara thoughtfully replied, "Joe, have you noticed a difference in Muffy?"

"Yeah, now that you mention it, she's gotten a lot quieter. It seems like she's thinking a lot."

Sara nodded. "Yes, but not just that. She watches us all the time, and she's become more helpful. I didn't even have to ask her to help with the dishes tonight."

Joe drawled, "The power of Jesus does change people, you know?"

"I know, I know. I'm just afraid that she'll leave Jesus here when she goes back home. We need to pray that she won't forget what she's learned here," Sara said worriedly.

"God can keep her, Sara. You know that," Joe said.

"You're right. I shouldn't worry, should I?"

As Joe put his book back on the shelf, Sara burst out, "But, Joe, what about—"

"Oh no, you don't. No fretting on Christmas Eve!" Joe interrupted. Come on. Let's go to bed, you worrywart!"

✳ ✳ ✳

Yawning and stretching, Muffy walked into the living room, where her cousins each ran to her and held out gifts. She quickly put her hands behind her back and said quietly, "But I don't have gifts for any of you."

Joe said, "That's all right. We don't give gifts to receive. We give because we love you."

Muffy repeated, "You love me?" In her shock she hardly heard the family affirming that they did indeed love her.

As usual, Billy was the one to break the tension. "Well, don't just stand there. Open your presents!"

"Mine first!" Emma said, then pushed a small package into Muffy's hands.

"Oh, Emma...a handkerchief embroidered with birds. It's lovely!"

Billy was next in line. "Now mine!"

Muffy opened the gift with shaking hands and exclaimed, "You made me a deer! Thank you! I'll keep it always!"

The final package contained two gifts. The knitted shawl was from Sara, and the hand-crafted copper box was from Joe. Choking out a muffled, "Thank you...thank you all," Muffy ran out of the room.

"Where did she go?" Emma asked, hurt feelings tightening her voice.

Billy asked, "Didn't she like her presents?"

"Joe, did it look like she was crying? Maybe I should go check on her." Sara's fretting was interrupted as Muffy burst back into the living room, her arms full of items.

"Billy, here...I want you to have this," she said and handed him a small bottle.

Looking doubtful, Billy said, "Uh...red stuff. Thanks?"

Muffy explained, "It's really rouge for my cheeks, but I thought you could use it to add color to your carvings."

With a nod of understanding, Billy enthusiastically said, "That's a good idea, Muffy! Thanks!"

Turning to her younger cousin, Muffy handed her a pink bonnet. "Emma, this is for you."

Emma protested, "Your bonnet...I can't take your fancy bonnet!"

Playfully, Muffy said, "It's not mine anymore. It's yours. So, don't argue!"

Next she handed her uncle Joe the music recording that he had liked. "I'll really enjoy it, Muffy. Thanks!"

With empty arms Muffy turned. "Aunt Sara, I want you to have this," she said before pulling off her pearl ring and handing it to her aunt.

Sara replied, "No, Muffy. I can't take your ring. That was a gift from your daddy."

Excitedly, Muffy responded, "Yes, you can! Ever since I got here, you all have been teaching me about giving. You gave me your time, you gave me your talents, and you gave me your love. Most importantly, you taught me about the best gift ever! I wouldn't have known about God's gift without you all, so please let me give something back to you!" Blinking back tears, she continued, "I want to tell you all that...I love you too."

Without really knowing how it happened, Muffy found herself suddenly surrounded. Everyone was crying and hugging until Billy wiggled free, saying, "I'm hungry! What's for breakfast?"

Evening in Paris

Cheryl Livingston

12/15/1950

My feet twisted back and forth in my cousin's hand-me-down saddle ox-fords as I gazed at the sparkling cobalt bottles. Each blue container, shim-mering in the harsh drug store lighting, was a small work of art, decorated with silver labels and sophisticated tassels. Gene Autry's voice, which was singing "Frosty the Snowman," faded away as I was transported to another place. The Eiffel Tower was behind me, and a handsome man was in front of me. He took me in his arms, leaned over me, and—

"Back again, hon?" The salesgirl's question interrupted my reverie. Her dangly red earrings bobbed in rhythm with her jaw as she chewed her gum. "Evening in Paris par-fum—that's about as romantic as it gets, right, hon? That would be a good Christmas present for your mom, hon!"

Embarrassed, I hurried away after giving her a shy nod. Evening in Paris for my mom? The thought dismayed me. It was for me, not her! But I guess the salesgirl only saw the insecure fourteen-year old in a too-big, frayed-around-the-edges plaid coat. Evening in Paris epitomized everything I wanted to be—beau-tiful, sophisticated, and worldly. Since I was none of those things, I hoisted my schoolbooks into a more comfortable position and daydreamed about my sweet-smelling future all the way home.

12/15/1951—Giggling, Elaine and I stood in front of the perfume counter, which was decorated with tiny, foil-wrapped boxes for the Christmas holidays.

Elaine was my newest and best friend. I was still amazed that someone as vibrant and popular as her wanted to be friends with me. We had met in Latin class, where I was dutifully conjugating verbs while she was busy flirting with Bobby Gene Wilson. When our grade cards came out for the first semester, I found her crying in the bathroom. Understandably, she had gotten a failing grade in Latin and was very close to failing Geography as well. In a burst of sympathy, I offered to be her tutor, since I did very well in both of those classes. Somehow, in spite of our differences, we bonded and became inseparable.

The friendly salesgirl from last year had been replaced with an older woman who frowned frequently in our direction, so we rarely tried on any of the scents, although she couldn't stop us from wistfully looking at the multi-hued containers. Elaine picked a different favorite every week. This week her choice was L'eur du Temps. It did have a beautiful bottle, with two lovebirds on the stopper, but as always, I remained loyal to those magical vessels of cobalt and silver.

I stopped Elaine in the middle of her lovebird imitation, which consisted of her arms swooping around the store, and told her I had to leave. My mom was working, and I needed to go home to make supper for my granddad. I had been embarrassed the first time she had come to my house, which was so different from her big, lovely home. But Elaine was not a snob, and she didn't even blink when she saw the worn upholstery and the tiny rooms of the shabby rental that I lived in with my mom and grandad. That's why it didn't bother me to ask, "Why don't you come with me, and we'll fix supper together? Afterwards, I can help you memorize the state capital cities for our test tomorrow."

Arms still swooping, she swung one of them around my shoulder and steered me toward the door. "That sounds super! After supper I'm finally going to beat your grandpa at Parcheesi!"

12/15/1952—Since I was in a rush, I didn't have time for my usual stop at the perfume display, but I did look at the new poster for Evening in Paris as I went by. This one was the best yet—a romantic concoction in tones of smoky blue. I sighed with longing. I wanted to travel the world, go to Paris, and learn to speak French. But instead, here I was in small town Elizabethton, Tennessee, buying Corn Huskers lotion for my grandad. I hoped that this time he wouldn't ask me to rub it on his feet.

12/15/1953—After school I met Elaine at the Woolworth's soda fountain, and she eagerly whispered, "Well, how did it go?"

The day before, we had surreptitiously applied a dab from the Evening in Paris sample bottle to each of our wrists. I had been about to go on my first date and had wanted to feel special. Elaine had set up a blind date with her cousin Elmer, who was from Johnson City. He took me to see the movie *Roman Holiday*, which starred Audrey Hepburn. In my mind she was the most beautiful creature on earth, but Elmer obviously hadn't felt the same way, because he whispered loudly in my ear during the whole movie.

"There won't be a second date!" I declared to Elaine. "He's a talker!"

"Hmmm..." she muttered. "Who could I introduce you to next? I know! Cousin Hank from Bristol!"

12/15/54—After Cousin Hank there had been Cousin Freddy: the burper, Cousin Eddy: the cougher, and Cousin Teddy: the complainer.

"Elaine, did your uncles deliberately tag their sons with rhyming names?" I asked listlessly as we were listening to "Mr. Sandman" on the record player in her room.

Ignoring my question, Elaine announced, "I have one more cousin for you! He just moved here from Newland, North Carolina. He doesn't know anyone, so it would be really nice if you went out with him."

Jumping off the bed, Elaine suddenly changed the subject, saying conspiratorially, "Mom's not home; she's at a Tupperware party. Let's go to her room and try on make-up."

Seeing my hesitation, she squashed my good-girl doubts with her next sentence. "She just bought the Evening in Paris powder!"

12/15/55—I looked over at the driver's seat to Daniel's handsome face and realized it was almost the one-year anniversary of our first date. Elaine's cousin from North Carolina had swept me off my feet by taking me to the Bonnie Kate Theater, where I had been thrilled to see that *Sabrina*, the new Audrey Hepburn movie, was playing. Afterward, we had shared hamburgers and fries at the Dutch Maid Drive-In. Getting our ice cream cones to go, we had driven through the Covered Bridge and talked. After just seeing a romantic movie, it had been easy to spill my dreams about someday going to France. His response had been, "Ginny, you could live in Paris. You remind me of Audrey Hepburn." I think I fell a little in love at that very moment.

12/15/56—My single mother and aging grandfather weren't able to help me, so my wedding day was not a big-budget affair. I hadn't even been able to afford my favorite perfume, but I was able to use my favorite color scheme. My silver brocade suit was accented perfectly by the brilliant blue heirloom brooch on my collar. A tiny hat with silvery feathers was perched on top of my freshly curled hair.

Elaine stood beside me in a frothy blue dress with a ribbon at the waist. She was making me giggle with her unique observations about life. "The man in the navy suit at the back of the church—his fluffy mustache makes him look like Captain Kangaroo!" she exclaimed, referencing a current children's television icon.

I glanced at the man in the back, but I couldn't take my eyes off of Daniel, who looked positively debonair (that's a French word that means distinguished and handsome). And on this wonderful day, I had never felt more beautiful. I felt…très jolie!

Instead of a honeymoon, we would be going to our cute little rented apartment, which was over Droke's shoe store on Elk Avenue. I couldn't wait to spend our first Christmas there—only ten days from now!

12/15/57—Smoothing my coat down over my ever-expanding belly, I gave only a cursory look toward the perfume counter. Our budget had nothing left over for perfume—or any Christmas gifts at all, for that matter. Daniel had a good job working at the hardware store for his father, but his salary was being stretched thin by the purchases we were making for the baby's nursery.

12/15/58—As a Christmas treat, Daniel took me to see *Funny Face* tonight. Even though it starred my favorite actress, it left me with coiling discontent in my belly. Audrey played the part of a girl who wanted to go to Paris, which reminded me of the dream that I had just recently locked away in a dark corner of my mind.

12/15/59—Daniel was completely confused as I burst into tears after the movie. He knew how I felt about France, so he thought I would love the movie *GiGi*. I explained it away as expectant-mother emotions, as our second baby was due any day. But just as my baby was alive inside me, so was my dream. And my dream wanted to live.

12/15/60—Who knew buying a house could be so expensive? No Christmas gifts for us this year!

12/15/61—A new alternator for our Chevy Bel Air gobbled up our Christmas budget this year.

12/15/62—No cobalt bottles under the tree for me this year. No trip to Paris either. A harvest-gold Frigidaire electric range will be my gift this year. Not that I mind, because there will be no Christmas turkey and no Christmas cookies until we get the new one installed.

12/15/63—Will we ever get on our feet financially? This year Christmas gifts will once again be on a shoestring. This time it's because my little Sabrina and Daniel Jr. both need glasses! They have appointments after the first of the year.

I have also decided that I am going to look for a job after the first of the year. This is a new era, and I am a modern woman! I can earn my own money!

12/15/64—Dr. Thomas said I could leave an hour early today. The downtown area was full of Christmas shoppers, but not many of those people were coming in for glasses. As I put on my coat, I thought, *What seemed like a financial catastrophe last Christmas was actually a blessing in disguise.* When I had taken the kids to Dr. Thomas to get their glasses, he had asked me to come back later for a job interview.

Taking advantage of my extra hour, I hurried down the street, going in the Kress store so I could get some small treats for the kids' stockings.

Fumbling with my keys at the front door, I was surprised when it opened in front of me. I was even more surprised when the small man in a suit and tie (that suspiciously looked like my Danny-boy with a fake mustache) took my coat and said, "Welcome, Madam. We haf your table weddy for you."

Yep, I thought, *that's my son, lisp and all!* Hiding my smile, I graciously followed him into the living room, where he led me under an archway that must have been made of every Lincoln Log, Tinker Toy, and building block the children owned.

On the other side of the "Arc de Triomphe," I found myself not in my living room but in a small Parisian café. Our black, wrought iron garden chairs had been brought inside and placed at a small café table, which was covered in a checkered spread. The breadsticks and two wine glasses were already at the center of the table, giving me a cheerful welcome. As I looked around, I realized that a slightly scratchy version of "La Mer" was playing on a portable record player. I knew the song well, as it was the old record that I had played hundreds of times as the background for my moony teenage dreams.

Danny-boy again reached up and took my arm. "Wet me help you with your seat," he said in his best grown-up voice.

As I was seated, I noticed a large, hand-lettered sign that announced the name of the restaurant as "Chez Petit Famille," with Sabrina's drawings of bread, wine, and spaghetti making a border around it. Where was Sabrina? I looked around and saw my daughter as she entered through the hallway door. She was wearing a long, silky dress that drug the ground behind her (was that my church dress!?), along with some pearls (and those are my grandmother's pearls!). Her hair was put up on her head in a fairly good approximation of a French knot, and she even had on a little lipstick (does Daniel know about the make-up?).

She glided over to me and kissed me on each check. "Velcome, darlink!" Oh dear, she sounded more like a female vampire than a French cabaret singer, but I appreciated her effort. At that point the music changed, and she began to lip-sync and sashay to "Thank Heaven for Little Girls," sung by Maurice Chevalier. Oh dear, this was so wrong in so many ways, and I struggled not to laugh. Fortunately, the song ended while I was still in control of myself, and I applauded loudly as she backed into the hallway and disappeared.

My next surprise came striding through the "Arc de Triomphe," and he was wearing a suit and tie and looking extremely handsome. My husband sat down across from me and apologized for his lateness with a wink that said, "It's all part of the plan." Our sommelier approached with a bottle of wine and carefully poured it into my glass while lisping, "Waydies fwoist!" Daniel and I shared a secret smile over the top of our little wine steward.

Sabrina brought us our menus, and this time she was dressed in a black and white striped top, a black skirt, and a red beret. The creatively crayoned menus gave me the limited options available: I could order spaghetti with sauce or spaghetti with meat balls. As we ate, Danny-boy "serenaded" us on his screechy beginner's violin. Oh dear, he really needed more lessons. As he finished his song, Sabrina presented our dessert—a plate of buttery madeleine cookies with lemon drizzle.

But the evening was not over yet. Daniel stood and asked me to walk with him. Arm-in-arm, we strolled back through the "Arc de Triomphe" and over to the wall of the coat closet, which had been transformed into a view of the Eiffel Tower by the application of a long photo poster.

"I have something for you," he said with a conspiratorial glance toward Sabrina and Danny-boy. "The kids and I wanted to give you the night in Paris that you always wanted, and this gift is part of it." I smiled as I tore through the wrappings, not expecting the wonderful item inside. Tears sprang to my eyes as I reverentially pulled the bottle of Evening in Paris perfume out of its cobalt and silver box.

"It's beautiful," I breathed.

"No, you're beautiful," my handsome date replied as took me in his arms and leaned me backwards into a passionate kiss.

My dream of being kissed in front of the Eiffel Tower was coming true! This time there was no salesgirl to stop my daydream, and there was no grandfather needing help to the bathroom to stop this wonderful—

"Ooh, yuck!" "Shooo!" The kids giggled, making their opinions known.

So my dream of the perfect kiss had been interrupted once again, but this time it was okay because this was better than any daydream I had ever had as that awkward fourteen-year old.

This was real life. It was my life. It was full of love, and it was good.

The Naked Christmas Tree

Linda Hudson Hoagland

Ellen slowly climbed out of the car as she looked up to see her naked Christmas tree shimmering like a ghost in her front window.

"I've got to take that tree down," she mumbled in disgust.

It was the last thing Aaron, her son, had done for her before he had moved away to another state, halfway across the country.

He had pulled the tree out of the storage box the day after Thanksgiving. The next day, Aaron and his girlfriend, Becky, had left for Nebraska.

Ellen had watched them drive away in the car that she had given them. They had been pulling a trailer filled with all of their worldly possessions. In her mind she had vowed that the tree would stay up until they returned.

She had stood there watching the car and the trailer fade away from her life while tears had slipped down her cheeks.

That day of departure had happened four years earlier, and that naked Christmas tree was still standing in the front window.

Mother's Day was coming, but Ellen knew there would be no happy celebration in her house.

Eddy, her eldest son, would be spending the day with his wife's mother, and, of course, Aaron was living in Nebraska.

Sonny, Ellen's husband and the stepfather of her two sons, was doing his best to make her happy on her day of celebration, but he figured he was fighting a losing battle. He had made a mistake when he told her, during a previous year, that since she was not his mother, he didn't see the need to buy her a card. That statement was one that he regretted.

"Come on, Ellen. Things will get better. Your boys will be here with you, hopefully, at Christmas. You know Aaron and Becky just can't drive here overnight, and they can't afford to jump in an airplane for a one day visit for Mother's Day," said her practical husband.

"I know, but it would be nice to see them here together. It has been four years, you know?" Ellen said sadly.

Ellen knew Sonny would want to watch the junior circuit of the NASCAR race, so she grabbed her crochet project and joined him in the living room.

"What's happening? I missed all the action when I went to get the angel that I'm crocheting," Ellen asked, feigning interest.

"Jeff Gordon and Dale Earnhart, Jr. got into a tangle and are both out of the race for now. I really don't think they will get back in, but I'll keep watching just in case," Sonny said with a happy laugh. He truly loved to watch the races, and he was a die-hard Earnhart, Jr. fan.

The circular motion of the race and the lack of crashes caused Sonny to drop off into a doze.

Ellen watched him sleep as she totally ignored the noisy television.

She cast her look up and said, "Thank you, God, for letting me have my Sonny for another day."

Sonny had a bad heart, and he could be taken away from her loving care at any time. Ellen was grateful for every moment he remained in her living room, in her tiny house, in her small town, and in her little corner of Appalachia.

❋ ❋ ❋

"You need to fill out an application for a Habitat House," said Patricia, a co-worker of Ellen's.

"I wouldn't get a house, Pat. Why bother?" Ellen asked. But she wanted so very much to get a house. Her mobile home was becoming a dangerous fire hazard, and she knew she would have to find a new place to live. With all of the medical expenses she had to come up with to keep Sonny alive, though, it was hard to do.

"I have an application right here. You and Sonny should fill this out, and you will already have two votes when the decision is made. My husband, Jimmy, and I are both on the selection committee," Patricia said with encouragement.

Sonny and Ellen completed the application and gave it to Patricia. They knew the process could take months, even years, so they accepted a long, unending wait.

The deterioration of their mobile home forced them to move without a Habitat house.

Because she worked in Tazewell, Ellen decided she needed to live closer to work so that if an emergency arose with Sonny's failing heart, it would be easier for her to get to him when he needed help.

Finally, a Habitat house became available, and they were approved to purchase it with affordable monthly payments.

That was how Ellen and Sonny came to own their little piece of Appalachia in Tazewell, Virginia.

Now she had her house, her Sonny, and two sons who had each married wonderful ladies.

Ellen was getting a little drowsy when there was a startling ring of the telephone, which was placed on a table next to Sonny's chair.

"Hello," he said in a raspy voice that was caused by a sudden awakening from his nap.

"Dad, don't let Mom know it's me. Tell her to go to the front door and open it. There is a Mother's Day present just outside the door."

"Okay, I will," Sonny said as he turned to Ellen. "There is a package waiting for you on the front porch."

"Who was that on the phone?" she asked as she rose from her chair.

"It was the delivery service. They wanted to make sure you knew it was there because it is perishable and they were a little late getting it here," he said with a grin that broke into a wide smile.

"What are you up to, Sonny?" Ellen asked as she reached for the doorknob, turning it and yanking the door open.

"Happy Mother's Day!" yelled four voices in unison.

Before her stood Aaron, Becky, Eddy, and Sherry.

"Mom, what are you going to do with that Christmas tree?" asked Aaron as he looked at the naked tree, which had been standing in the front window since he had left four years earlier.

"We're going to decorate it while you're here. It will stay there until you come back for another visit to remove the decorations."

"That means Becky and I have to return at Christmas, doesn't it?"

"Yes," Ellen said with a motherly smile.

The Christmas tree had been in the front window through season after season, with all of the decorations placed on the tree exactly how the kids had left them when they were together and at home.

"Mom, Becky and I will be moving back to Virginia by Christmas this year, we hope," Matt said excitedly.

"Really? Why?" Ellen asked with equal excitement.

"The cost of living in Omaha is about to kill us. We need to get back to where things are normal," he explained.

"I can't wait to see you two again," Ellen said happily. "Just let me know when you're coming so I can get your room ready."

That call occurred in midsummer.

The next call was to let her know that they had not finished the repairs to the house, so it would most likely be in the spring before they would be moving back to Virginia.

Another call from Aaron said, "We should be there by the end of January, for Becky's birthday. I have located a small fixer-upper house on Baptist Valley Road. I need you to go look at it and see if you think it would be good enough for us to move into the day we get there. We need to find a place where we can unload the truck into the new place, if you know what I mean. I have to get the truck back to the rental place," he explained in a stream of words.

"Email me the address and the real estate agent's name so I can make an appointment to see the place," Ellen instructed him. "Do you really think you will be here soon?"

"The buyers want our house, but we have to wait to see if the financing goes through."

"I hope so."

Ellen moved bookcases and boxes from the spare bedroom so that Aaron and Becky could rest their heads when they arrived. That was a task that took several days and a lot of heavy lifting.

There was a flurry of phone calls updating Ellen on the progress that was being made in Omaha.

About a week before the planned time to get on the road with the loaded truck, the call came to Ellen saying that the sale of the house fell through. They couldn't leave yet.

Ellen was crushed.

"What's the plan now?" Ellen asked Aaron.

"We have to wait for another buyer. The last one didn't go through, because the man's wife was an illegal alien. The lender was a FHA (Federal Housing

Authority) loan, and they wouldn't, or couldn't, finance the purchase of the house if the man's wife had the possibility of being deported," he explained angrily.

"I'm so sorry, honey."

"Me too," he said in an angry, tear-choked voice.

Ellen was waiting once again, with a decorated Christmas tree in her front window and an empty spare room.

It will happen, she thought as she said a prayer, crossed her fingers, and forced herself to smile.

An Un-Merry Day

Linda Hudson Hoagland

I could hear the pitter-patter of little feet where there should be no pitter-patter of little feet.

The noise was right over my head, in the attic that consisted of a small crawl space, which was definitely not a room big enough to be functional for anything other than the storage of boxes that would be carried up there and forgotten.

I strained my concentration, focusing on the sound.

"Footsteps," I mumbled. "It sounds like a little person walking around over my head. I know it can't be. There are no little people living in this house."

Being the wizened age of sixty-six, the sound of the pitter-patter of the feet of small children was long gone. My two boys had never fathered young ones, so the sounds of grandchildren were never present.

"Rats," I mumbled.

The sounds dissipated, and my mind jumped to another topic.

"I've got to find my Christmas decorations. I hope they are not in the attic," I mumbled as I looked in the hall closet, which was packed with storage boxes.

Mumbling or outright talking to myself had become an everyday occurrence since the passing of my husband. I was alone so much of the time that the only voices I would hear came from the television or my own mouth.

I hate to contradict those professionals who claim to know so much, but not all people who talk to themselves are crazy. Some of them, like me, are just plain lonely.

I kept the television on to fill the house with people sounds. It made the house feel warmer and more inviting.

I looked at the boxes in the hall closet. I was going to have to open each one of them to find what I was looking for. That was going to be a back-breaking job, and the Christmas decorations might not even be in there.

I was not really that forgetful, but I hadn't been at home when my son and his wife had taken the Christmas decorations down and packed them away somewhere during the previous holiday season. I had forgotten to ask where they were when I got back home, and I certainly wasn't going to ask them now. I just assumed they had placed them in the hall closet or another closet in the house.

The boxes were stacked to the top in both ends of the tiny storage room. That only allowed room in the center portion to hang jackets or coats. I emptied the center portion of hanging items and piled them on the floor.

Then I realized I needed the step stool to safely get to the top box. I located the step stool in the kitchen and carried it to the hallway.

"There it is again," I said as I stopped dead to listen. I stood there, not moving an inch. I ran to turn down the sound on the television, and I found myself holding my breath so I could better hear the pitter-patter.

Nothing—no sounds were heard.

"It's just your imagination, Ella Grace," I mumbled as I proceeded on my way to the closet.

It took me over two hours to pull each box from its position, open the lid, and set it to the side, only for it to be re-stacked later.

I was too tired to tackle the next closet search, so I went to the living room to rest for a bit.

I normally wanted the television on to drown out the outside world, but this time I wanted the silence.

I stretched out on the sofa and closed my eyes. I didn't want to go to sleep. As my dad always told me, "I just want to rest my eyes." And then the rafter-rattling snores would start. I figured I was a lot like my father even without the loud snoring—at least I hoped so.

The noises over my head infiltrated my dreams. I saw rats. They were huge, giant, big rats, and they were racing back and forth in a small, attic-like room. The size of the creatures was disproportionate to the size of the room, so when they ran, they had to duck their ugly heads, just like I would have to do in my attic. The pitter-patter stopped, but now there were heavy footsteps that slapped against the rough wood flooring that covered my ceiling of sheetrock.

I must have climbed up the folding stairway, which allowed me access to the attic, because I was up there, playing, smiling, and talking with them as if I were very happy to do so. We joined hands—perhaps I should say claws—bent forward to keep from hitting our heads on the rafters, and circled around as if we were listening to some peculiar music.

When the rats raised their heads up, they had to sit back on their haunches so there would be no head-banging pain. They would throw their heads back and bare their teeth, and I could have sworn it looked like they smiled.

When they stopped whirling around, I had to stop, but I had to bend my knees as I raised my head, bared my teeth, and smiled. That little dance continued until a frenzy caused the gnashing of teeth, and the smiles turned to grimaces of attack.

It was time to go when that happened, or I would have become the makings for the next meal.

I ducked down and backed away toward the folding staircase, which would lead me to safety.

Suddenly the opening to safety was closed, and the three gnarling, gnashing rats were coming toward me. Their eyes were red, and the spittle was dripping from their mouths.

"Back off! Get away!" I screamed as I ran to the folding staircase, which would lead me to the floor below and to the escape from my dream.

The snarling rats kept coming, and I couldn't get the trap door open. It was as if someone were on the other side pushing up and holding it securely in place.

"Help!" I screamed.

The rats kept coming.

"Help me, please!" I cried.

The rats lunged at me, and I squirreled back as far as I could go until I hit my head against a really low rafter, and then—

I sat up, blinked my eyes, and glanced around the room as I pulled my angel afghan up to my chin.

"It was only a dream," I mumbled as I crawled from my sofa in search of normalcy. I remembered why I didn't nap during the daylight hours.

"There it is again," I whispered as I walked to the bathroom. "So help me, there is something up there walking around," I continued loudly. I must have wanted the noise makers to know that I knew they were there. I just couldn't imagine how rats could get into my attic, and I had no idea what they were feeding on to stay alive.

I tried to ignore the pitter-patter. I turned my television sound up louder, but when I did that, I still strained harder and harder to hear the sounds.

I knew I was going to have to go check out the attic all by myself. One of my sons lived out of state, and the other one was at work. I had no one to call to give me a helping hand.

"Suck it up, Ella Grace, and go check out the attic," I told myself in a scolding tone.

I dragged the step stool back into the hallway, climbed up, and tugged on the rope handle that was dangling from the door to the loftier heights.

I pulled at the rope slowly. I must have been afraid something would jump at me.

I saw something move, so I let go of the rope handle and pushed up against the door, watching it spring into place flush against the ceiling.

I climbed down from the step stool and ran to the living room, where I plopped myself down on the sofa, clutching at my chest.

I took slow, steady breaths to calm myself down and to stop my heart from racing.

"I hear it again," I said to anyone that could hear me.

Of course, no one heard me.

I was alone, as usual, except for whatever was walking around on my ceiling.

My breathing had returned to normal, and the pain in my chest had subsided. I stood up, took a deep breath, and walked back to the hallway, where I stared at the step stool to horror.

I climbed up on the step stool, pulling at the rope handle as I closed my eyes.

I felt the metal stairs begin to slide down.

I opened my eyes and peered into the gaping hole.

I stepped off the stool and onto the metal ladder. I hurried up the metal contraption because I was afraid I would back out of checking on the attic.

My line of vision came up to the floor/ceiling, where I gazed across the room to search out the noise makers. Only my head was actually through the hole and into the attic. That was how I wanted to keep it.

I saw two stuffed toys leaning against the wall. It looked as if a spotlight were shining on them. I don't know what I was expecting to see, but it certainly wasn't two stuffed toys.

Then...I saw them move. I was not crazy. I saw them move. They were walking toward me.

I jerked back from what I was seeing and totally lost my balance, which caused me to fall to the floor.

I wasn't sure how long I was out, unconscious from banging my head when it hit the floor.

I was sitting up when my son knocked at the door.

"Mike, use your key. I can't get to the door," I shouted as I rubbed the back of my head, which was bleeding a bit.

I heard the keys rattle against the door as he unlocked it, opening the door slowly. He was afraid of what he would find on the other side of that door.

"Mom, what happened?" he asked as he ran to me.

"I was looking for the Christmas decorations. I thought they were in the attic. Is that where you and Sherry put them last year?" I asked. I didn't want to tell him that I had heard the pitter-patter of footsteps in the attic.

"No, they are in the back bedroom closet. You should not be climbing around on things when you are alone. Call me the next time. Okay?" he said sternly.

"Oh, okay," I said. "Before you close up the steps, would you go get the stuffed toys that are up there? I want to give them away," I said as I continued to rub at the back of my head.

"Is that what you were after?" he asked.

"Well, no. I was looking for the Christmas decorations," I snapped back at him.

"I need to take you to the emergency room," he said as he helped me up from the floor.

"No, I'll be okay. The bleeding has stopped. But please get those toys for me," I pleaded.

Mike climbed up the steps. I could hear him walking around.

"Where are the toys?" he asked.

"Look behind some of the boxes," I shouted. "They may have gotten shoved to the back." I knew they had not been shoved anywhere. They had actually walked there.

"Here they are," he said as he threw them down the steps, causing them to land close to my feet. He then climbed down the steps and closed the door to the attic.

"Mom, you need to go to the emergency room," he cajoled.

"I'll go take a shower and wash my hair. If the cut on my head is still bleeding after that, I'll go to the emergency room with you. How does that sound?" I asked.

"I'll wait right here until you get out of the shower," he said hesitantly.

I had a bit of a headache, but the bleeding had stopped. I knew a hospital trip was not needed.

Once I climbed from the shower and showed Mike that there was no more blood, he went on his way. I didn't even know why he stopped by the house, and he never did tell me.

I located my scissors and made quick work of cutting up the stuffed toys before shoving them into a garbage bag and carrying them outside to rest in peace.

I decided to let the Christmas decorations stay in the closet in the back bedroom. I didn't think I wanted to celebrate any more of that un-merry day.

New Member of the Family

Lori C. Byington

Even though the Channel 5 weatherman had warned that there would be snow, the mid-December day dawned with the sun in full bloom, and the sky is that deep color of blue that makes the plumes of the summer blue jays seem dim. Myrtle Counts stands in the driveway of the white house that she has lived in for too many years to count. The home she and Tal (Talmadge) built so many years ago is on the outskirts of Bristol, Tennessee, and they have just finished a breakfast of over-easy fried eggs, bacon from the hog Tal had butchered last fall, and homemade cat-head biscuits, which were compete with delectable apple butter that was courtesy of Bear Hollow United Methodist Church. Tal, her husband of more than 30 years, is about to go to town for their weekly groceries and random supplies like light bulbs, Dawn dish soap, a battery to fix the old green Oliver tractor, and, as usual, a bag of corn for the small herd of deer, which are more like pets than wildlife.

He hesitantly asks, "Do you know of anythin' else we need from White's?" He knows she always comes up with something essential at the last minute.

She unnecessarily reminds him, "Don't forget the deer corn! The girls will be on the back porch if that feeder isn't full."

Tal nods, smiles, and promises, "Don't worry. That four-year-old is a bit friendly, and she WILL head bump me if I don't pour the corn fast enough. Oh, and watch Rosie, the Hereford, in the barn. She was a bit antsy yesterday, and with the full moon, that early calf may come before we know it!"

Myrtle nods and promises, "I will check right after lunch."

After a kiss straight on Myrtle's chapped lips, Tal heaves himself into his silver Ford F250 truck, starts the engine, puts the vehicle in reverse, and backs out of the drive. Gray smoke from the exhaust reminds Tal that a tune-up at Pond Creek Auto is long overdue.

Myrtle yells at the last minute, "Be careful! I love you!" Tal grins and blows a kiss to his beloved, then downshifts into gear to head to town.

After Tal drives away, Myrtle glances around to admire the evergreen garland and the Oxford blue and forest green bows that drape across the banister and the railing of the front porch. She pauses and thinks, *The smell of the air right before snow falls is the best smell in the world.* Actually, a bit hopeful, Myrtle recalls what was said on the news earlier in the morning on WHBL. Johnny Moore, the local weather reporter, had reported a cold front and snow to be likely. Myrtle looks to the sky and sees that fluffy, cumulous clouds have taken over the once fierce blue sky. Out of nowhere the wind, crisp and clean, picks up. The swift breeze looks otherworldly as it wafts through the pine trees and over the first frost-laced grass like ancient ghosts who are long overdue for an outing. Myrtle looks to the heavens, prays a selfish prayer for wonderful snow on Christmas, and breathes in deeply. Her nose hairs freeze on the first inhale as the air forms ice crystals that stick in her nostrils. An unanticipated sneeze breaks the quietness of the moment, and Myrtle shakes her gray-blond head. All of a sudden, tiny, wispy, delicate, white flakes land on her eyelashes. She blinks twice and then looks up. Sure enough, Johnny had been right! The promised snow has begun! Other than the time of the winter solstice, there is no other season that comes close to a crazy obsession for her. *I love winter in the East Tennessee mountains,* she muses.

About twenty minutes after leaving the house, Tal pulls in at White's Mercantile. His trips to White's are legendary. A week never goes by without him taking at least three ventures to Bristol's fabulous mercantile. "If we don't have it, then you don't need it," is the motto painted on the side of the barn-like building. Although the slogan on the green storefront is a bit faded after years of weather, the message still rings true for locals and anyone who chances to visit the area.

Tal gets out of the truck and notices there are more cars than usual in the parking lot. *What in the world?* goes through his mind. In an instant the front door flies open with a bang, and Jamie—White's longtime errand boy, all around helper, and cherished grandson—bounds down the steps, a box perched perilously on his right shoulder.

Without pausing in his lanky strides, he gasps, doffs his faded King College baseball cap, and breathes out, "Hey, Mr. Counts! How you doin'?" Jamie pauses at his trustworthy but dented Tundra 4x4 and plops the box into the bed of the truck. Taking a big breath, he looks at Tal like he has three heads.

Tal frowns and responds, "Fine, Jamie. What in the world is goin' on? And why are you lookin' at me like I am crazy, and why are you in such a hurry?"

"Well, didn't you see the news this morning? There's a big one headin' this way, and the weatherman said we'd get up to six inches of snow...at least!" Jamie spurts out. "See! The downpour has already started! I have to get these groceries to Mrs. Hall before she has a hissy fit. Calls are comin' in left and right! We are slammed with grocery deliveries. I guess everyone wants Kern's bread, Farmbest milk, and Jiff peanut butter! I have to get going. See you later!" Jamie whoops as he leaps into his Tundra, quickly starts the engine, and speeds off out of the parking lot.

Tal shakes his grizzled head and starts to head into White's. Before he goes in the door, he looks at the gray, cloud-filled sky, and, sure enough, dime-sized snowflakes have started to float down like feathers from teenagers' pillow fights. As he walks in and heads to the battery and mechanic section, old man White bellows from the produce section, "Hey, Tal...what do you need? I want to close before the snow gets too deep and I can't get home. My Michelins have needed a changin' since last winter."

Tal nods and relays, "I need a battery for my old Oliver, deer corn, and some groceries, but I can get the battery later. Is the snow really goin' to get deep? I don't recollect Johnny sayin' so in his weather report." Tal starts to chortle and continues, "Course, he never gets much weather right—at least not when I need the rain."

Mr. White's face betrays what he really feels. "Tal, I am afraid of this one. I have a feelin' in my bones. My right knee is givin' me a fit, so I am goin' to trust the clouds and the snow comin' down right now," he admits.

"Oh! Alright then. I'll get the corn, some bread, and Jiff...just in case we get snowed in," Tal promises. He walks hastily through the aisles and grabs some random items, along with the bread and peanut butter. Mr. White shouts from another aisle, "Don't worry none about payin' now. I will put the ticket in the drawer. You can pay later."

Tal thanks Mr. White and helps him lock up the store. Sure enough, the snow has really started to come down. The pillowcase feathers have turned into quarter-sized discs, and the "quarters" have started to stick to the ground with a vengeance. At least a three-inch start of what looks to be twelve or more inches of the fluff has fallen in the 45 minutes while Tal had been in White's. Tal worries to himself, *I hope Mr. White makes it home safely, and I hope that calf has not decided to grace the world early. Please let Myrtle be okay.*

Myrtle piddles around the house and adds treasured Christmas decorations to the tree and banisters. Her decoration colors of blue, green, and silver are hand-me-downs from her mother, Martha, and her grandmother Elizabeth. Most of the tree decorations are heirlooms that are over 100 years old. As she places each blue ball and crystal bell on the sturdy pine branches of their Christmas tree, she fondly remembers the wonderful traditions she and Tal had created themselves. Honestly, Tal gave the color choices of decorations to Myrtle. She chuckles and thinks, *He has no sense of design, but he does have an eerie sense of animals and crops.*

"Oh crap!!" Myrtle realizes. "I have to check on Rosie!" During her reverence of the early snow and the love of decorating for Christmas, Myrtle had completely forgotten about the poor momma cow. She runs to the door and struggles to put on her green Carhartt winter coat. Then she grabs her UVA beanie and a pink scarf that a fellow breast cancer survivor had knitted for her, and she stumbles into her blue, pink, and green Tractor Supply rubber boots. When she opens the door, a whoosh of wind and swirling snowflakes slap her in her face. The snow flurries had turned into a downright deluge, and at least five or six inches had gathered on the frozen yard. Wiping flakes away from her eyes, Myrtle looks toward the faded red barn, and it seems like it is a mile away. She makes first tracks into the fluffy mounds and trudges to the barn to see about Rosie.

Myrtle tries to quietly slide open the barn door, but an old barn and rusty rails and hinges do not quite cooperate "quietly." An eerie *squeeeeeeek* breaks the peacefulness of the falling snow, and Myrtle pushes the door open just enough to slide through. *I need to remind Tal to grease that door,* Myrtle mentally notes. She is met with a deep bellow from Rosie, who is apparently overjoyed to see one of her humans. Myrtle notices how cozy the barn is, even during the small blizzard going on outside. She slides the barn door closed and walks about ten feet inside, going to Rosie's stall. Standing on her tippy toes, Myrtle peeps over the stall door to look at the patient.

"There, there, girl. I'm here to check on you and your big belly," assures Myrtle.

Myrtle raises the door latch and opens the stall door. It, too, needs some WD-40. Myrtle is met by another "MMMMAAAAA!" from Rosie. Myrtle looks around the stall and then sees Rosie reach her head around to bite at her bulging flanks. The miserable cow is clearly in pain.

"Oh, poor girl," Myrtle coos. "I'm here." She rubs Rosie's soft, brown and white head, and Rosie responds with a hard butt against Myrtle's outstretched hand. Rosie stomps her right foot, and puffs of sawdust and straw rise like tiny ghosts. She begins to walk in circles but pauses every now and then to bite at her belly and stomp her foot. Myrtle begins to feel up and down Rosie's large belly and suddenly feels a hard kick from within. "Oh heavens!" she exclaims. "I guess the little one is not going to wait much longer!" Myrtle frowns and pushes her gray-blond curls out of her face. "Well, I sure don't know what to do, but I guess Tal will be along shortly," she half-promises to Rosie. *I hope he gets home soon*, she muses. She is not panicked...yet.

Myrtle decides to try to get to the house so she can call Tal to check on him. As she pushes open the squeaky barn door, both a gust of wind and mounds of snow welcome her and block her path. "Goodness gracious, what a beautiful sight!" she exclaims. "Oh dear! I hope Tal can get home!"

Immediately, Rosie gives a heart rendering caterwaul that shakes Myrtle to the bone. "Lord God tomatoes! She's having that baby!" Myrtle squeals—not that anyone can hear her, but hopefully God and St. Francis take notice. She decides better of heading to the house, so she closes the barn door so she can see about Rosie. She feels the chill of Jack Frost and stuffs her hands into her pockets.

Rosie lets out another loud "WHOOOAAA," and Myrtle hustles to the stall and finds the cow pacing and adamantly pawing the stall floor. Rosie flips her regal head around once again to bite at her distended belly. Myrtle looks, and her mouth falls open in an unaired gasp. "The baby moved!" Myrtle blurts without breathing. "Oh dear! What am I supposed to do?" Without a hint of warning, Rosie flops down and nips her belly again. She is obviously in labor.

Myrtle frets, *What do I need? What do I do? Clean towels? Forceps?* An audible "UGGGG" escapes from Rosie, and Myrtle runs to the storage room to see what she can use to help birth a calf. She fishes through piles of burlap, hay bale strings, and old Southern States sweet feed bags, but she finds nothing she might call sanitary or comfortable. "Oh gracious!" Myrtle shrieks. "What am I going to do to help Rosie?" Myrtle's exclamation is met with another "WHOOOAAA," and she strides quickly back to Rosie's stall. Myrtle glances around while in panic mode and feels as useless as boobs on a boar-hog.

All at once, Rosie groans and water gushes out of her backside. "That baby is coming whether I am ready or not," Myrtle admits. She looks around for extra sawdust and bunches up some near Rosie's rear end. Another groan from Rosie alerts Myrtle. Rosie bites at her flank again but then lies over, out of breath. Her breathing becomes labored, and she snorts every now and then. Rosie bellows "UUUUUU" and raises her head again. Myrtle senses something is wrong and kneels beside Rosie. "There, there, girl. I am here," Myrtle coos softly. The momma calms a bit, but not for long. Soon Rosie bellows and gives a grunt. "Heavens above! I don't have anything to help Rosie or anything to put the calf in," Myrtle laments. Rosie snorts in response, as if to say, "Do something!"

Ten minutes pass, and although Rosie has tried, she still has not birthed her calf. Myrtle wonders, *What if the calf is breach? Oh, dear Noah's Ark, what am I to do?* As if to answer, Rosie gives a loud "UUMMMMPH," and a tiny, brown, fuzzy head pops out of her back end. Myrtle scrambles to Rosie and waits impatiently for Rosie to push again. Within seconds Rosie grunts, and a bit more of the baby oozes out. The baby is covered in slime, as if he or she were from *Ghostbusters*, but to Myrtle's dismay, the whole body does not come out. Rosie grunts again, but this time it's a little softer. The poor momma is bone-tired. Minutes go by, and Rosie has not moved much. Myrtle notices and frowns enough to cause her blue eyes to fade into her knit brows. On the verge of panic, Myrtle asks the heifer, "What is going on, girl?" In response Rosie grunts a little, but the calf only slides out an inch. An unexpected calm comes over Myrtle, and she realizes she has to help Rosie deliver her baby.

A light bulb goes off in Myrtle's head. She jumps up and goes to the storeroom to grab some baling twine and sweet feed sacks. The bags still have the smell of molasses and oats, and the smell calms Myrtle a bit. When she goes back into Rosie's stall, Rosie grunts again. The wee calf is still not out, and time is flying by. Myrtle clucks softly to Rosie and kneels down behind her haunches. Myrtle then cautiously wipes the slime off of the baby's nose and, on a whim, guardedly starts to feel back into Rosie's body to see how much more the calf's body is inside. Myrtle reckons, *I have seen Tal help a calf and foal to be born. I guess I can too.* As she eases her hand along the calf's body, Rosie fusses. "Oh goodness, baby. You are not making this easy on your momma or me." Rosie lets out a "MMMAAAA" again, and the calf shudders a bit but does not move anywhere near the freedom from his momma's insides.

In her heart Myrtle knows what she has to do. "I have to pull that baby out of its momma." She nods to Rosie. With fierce tenaciousness Myrtle gathers the baling twine and folds over to double the rough strands. She takes a sweet feed bag and wraps the twine around it to make a sling. As the Southern States logo on the feed bag glares at her, Myrtle eases the contraption around the part of the calf's body that has seen daylight. "Okay, little one. I have to help you and your momma, so don't hate me if I hurt you a bit," Myrtle tells the calf. Rosie lifts her head as if to question Myrtle, but then she gives an "OOOMPH" and lies back down.

Myrtle takes a deep breath and silently asks again for God and St. Francis to help. She begins to pull easily on the calf. The baby inches out a bit, and Rosie groans. Feeling elated at her device, Myrtle pulls again, ever so gently. The baby moves out more, and Rosie gives a strong "MMMAAAA." Exhilarated, Myrtle pulls again, a bit harder this time, but the baby does not budge. She sits back on her butt and takes a deep breath. *Do I need to do something else?* she wonders as she half-closes her blue-gray eyes. Rosie slaps her tail in Myrtle's face as if to tell her, "hurry up!" Myrtle's hands are getting red because of the thin baling twine, and her fingers burn. She has a notion and grabs a Kleenex out of her coat pocket, wrapping it around the twine. Determined, Myrtle gets behind Rosie and the baby again. She grabs the twine and Kleenex and commands, "Okay, baby. It's time to meet your momma!" She takes one last inhale and pulls harder in order to free the baby. As she tugs hard on the makeshift sling, without a how do you do, the calf pops out of his momma like the cork out of a pop-gun from Mast General Store. The momentum causes Myrtle to fly backwards in the air, and she lands right in a stinky, fresh cow pile. As she overcomes her shock, Myrtle takes no notice of her noxious situation and crawls over to the calf to wipe off the slime and unhook her contraption. The calf loudly snorts snot into Myrtle's face, and Myrtle laughs out loud with relief and happiness.

Rosie gives a calming "MOOOO" and weakly stands up. She gingerly saunters over to her newborn and begins to lick the brown and white baby boy. The young one tries to stand, but his wobbly legs don't work yet.

Myrtle props against the stall wall and basks in the glow of a newborn. Abruptly, but a bit late, the barn door bursts open. Snowflakes fly in like whirling dervishes. A whoosh of air runs down the barn hall and carries Tal's worried words. "Myrtle! Are you here? Are you okay?" he hollers. Myrtle pushes herself up to her knees and makes her way to an upright position. "Yes! I'm fine," she calls back. She sticks her head out of Rosie's stall and meets Tal with a grin as big as the one from the Cheshire Cat in *Alice in Wonderland.* Tal rushes over and hugs his bride over the stall door.

"What have you been doing? I called, but you didn't answer, and I got worried! I got stuck helping Mr. White get out of a snow pile, and I could not drive fast because of the storm," Tal jabbers. Myrtle grins and nods in the direction of Rosie. "I'll have you know I have birthed a baby!" she brags. Tal's gaze finds the new momma, and, low and behold, there is a wee, brown and white calf trying to steady himself on spindly legs.

"Well, how do you like that!" Tal grins as wide as the barn door he just rushed through. He turns to Myrtle, "How'd ya do it?" Myrtle grins, her blue eyes sparkle, and she confidently tells Tal, "Well, I made a sling and helped Rosie have her baby." Tal shakes his head in wonderment, and flakes of snow fall out of his gray hair. "You always have been the strong one in the family. Rosie is glad too," Tal admits.

The couple hug and admire the newest member of the Counts family. Impulsively, Myrtle laughs with relief and winks. "Did you get the deer corn?"

CHANGES

Priscilla Arnold

Lily Hayes gazed out the window, watching as the snow peppered the ground. Six months ago, her world had changed irretrievably when her husband had sunk to the flagstone patio after having a massive heart attack. That day was imbedded deep in her brain with his passing. In the blink of an eye, her happy existence became desolate.

Astin had been a wonderful man, and she had always looked forward to their days together. Since his retirement, he had cooked their meals when she worked late at the law office. These days, to keep from starving, she learned how to cook and even tried her hand at baking. Her scones would never win first prize in a baking contest, but they were palatable. Also, he had taken over the tedious tasks of the laundry and grocery shopping.

No longer was she the dependent woman who leaned on her husband. She rarely went into the office—and not because of the deep snow that made it difficult to get off of the eastern Tennessee mountain. When she graduated from college, she opted for law school because she wanted to help innocent people. After several years of working as a lawyer, defending people left a bitter taste in her mouth. To plead a case in an effective manner, the defendant must divulge all the facts. Her last case was extremely difficult. The defendant kept important information from her and lied to her. He wasn't the first defendant who made her job hard. Her zest for her work changed from her original expectation when she left law school to humdrum.

With Astin's passing, her partners volunteered to work her legal cases until she returned. She received calls from them weekly, and then they came almost daily. Their concern was touching at first, but as time passed, they wanted a return date. She saw their point. They carried her for six months, and it was time for her to either return to the firm or resign. She didn't need to worry about finances, as Astin's investments left her well off. Though, if she resigned, what would she do? When not at the law office, she dabbled in her favorite hobby: painting landscapes. Gina, a friend, offered to display the paintings in her art gallery. She always put her off. In further contemplation the idea of exhibiting her paintings appealed to her. If no one took an interest in her work, so be it. Showing her paintings and quitting her job meant a new beginning. She set her cup of chamomile tea on the table and called Gina, who expressed her delight.

Then she punched in the phone number for the law office. "I won't keep you hanging any longer. I have made my decision," she said to Harry, the senior partner.

"Hold on, Lily. I'm in the conference room with the other partners. I'll put you on speakerphone."

She paused.

"Go ahead, Lily."

"You've all been gracious in giving me the strength to carry on after losing Astin, along with the time to reflect on my future. Through the years, you've treated me well, and I hope I've lived up to your expectations as a trial lawyer. Working as a lawyer has been good for me in many ways. But in recent years I've struggled, and I've lost the satisfaction each case once gave me. With this said, I'm resigning."

"I'm not surprised by your decision, as I'm aware of your struggles. I've enjoyed working with you, and you're a fine lawyer. Also, I wish you good luck and happiness in whatever new endeavor you undertake."

"Thank you for the kind words. In a few days I'll come into the office for my personal possessions and sign off...weather permitting." The other lawyers extended their best wishes as well before clicking off. A feeling of freedom swept over her.

She glanced outside at the snow falling and groaned. How soon would she be able to drive down the mountain? She clicked on the television and punched the channel for the weather on the remote. The meteorologist forecasted snow for the next two to three days. Frowning, she sipped her now cold tea and set the cup in the sink.

Upstairs, she pictured Astin building her perfect studio. Tears filled her eyes, and she swiped at them. By tapping into his carpentry skills, he had built shelves and created a wooden structure with drawers so she could store her paints and display the canvasses. She and Astin had selected this room for the lighting and the spectacular views. Huge windows faced the garden in her backyard. Each spring, the flowers bloomed, providing an array of exquisite colors. Beyond, a creek flowed when not iced over.

To her surprise a deer with a large rack of antlers meandered over to the creek from the evergreen of the trees. The animal lowered its head and licked on the ice. The deer twitched its head, glanced around, and bounded into the trees. She moved to her easel and stared at the unfinished painting of a deer leaping in a meadow. With the tip of a brush, she dabbed at the brownish-gray paint on her palette and lightly touched the deer. She painted until her stomach rumbled, and then she dropped the brush into the jar of paint thinner.

In the kitchen she lifted a chicken and broccoli casserole from the refrigerator and set it in the oven for warming. She gathered fixings for a tossed salad. Outside, darkness fell. Once she ate her evening meal and washed the dishes, she went to her bedroom. Lying in bed, she thought of her decision to quit law and to begin to paint. Painting made her happy, but the downside was that she lived in a cocoon. She rarely met with friends, since they lived closer to town than she did, and her daughter, Sami Lynn, lived in Nashville. Maybe she should sell the house and move off the mountain. But how could she leave the home where she and Astin spent twenty-five happy years?

She drifted off to sleep and was later awakened by a slight noise. Had someone broken in? What kind of person wanders around in a snowstorm? The whole scenario was unlikely because she lived so far up the mountain. The closest neighbor lived at least half a mile down the winding road. And Sami Lynn had other plans.

She donned her robe and crept downstairs. The sound came from the kitchen. Something scratched on the backdoor and whined. It wasn't human. She breathed a sigh of relief. She flipped the light switch on. Opening the inside door, she glanced down. On the patio a shivering dog stared at her. Snow covered its body. "Oh, you poor thing!" Opening the outside door, the small dog wandered in. "Where did you come from? No collar either." She opened a cupboard and grabbed a small, chipped bowl. At the sink she filled the dish with water and set it on the floor. The dog sipped the water. At the refrigerator she removed a platter of roast beef. She sliced and diced pieces of the meat and placed the food in a plastic container.

While the dog ate, she ran upstairs and scrounged in a closet. She snatched a towel and a pillow. After drying the dog, she sat back on her haunches. "You're a beautiful bluish-gray and tan color, which means you're a Yorkshire terrier. And you're not shivering. I bet your owner is missing you like crazy." She stood. Once the dog was settled on the pillow, she turned off the kitchen light.

She went to bed, and the whining began again. She rose and turned the light switch on. At the foot of the stairs, the dog stared pitifully at her. Shaking her head, she went downstairs, reached for the pillow, and held the dog in her other arm. After making a place near the bed for the dog, she sank into the mattress and slept. At dawn the dog barked, and she turned over. The dog paced to the top of the stairs. "I suppose you need to go outside." The cutie stared at her. "What should I call you?" She grimaced. "Does Jane work for you?" The dog looked solemn, and she slipped on her robe while the dog waited. "The stairs make you nervous?" Lily asked while lifting Jane. At the back door the dog hesitated a second before scrambling into the snow.

Lily closed the door and walked to a cabinet. She grabbed a bowl and a box of cold cereal. In a few minutes the yelping commenced. She opened the door and smiled. Jane ran inside and shook her coat, spraying water around the kitchen. Lily grabbed a sponge mop from the utility closet and dried the floor. "I need to take you to the veterinarian for an examination," she said. The dog cricked its head toward her and turned to its water bowl, slurping.

While she filled a bowl with shredded wheat, she gazed out the window at the huge snowflakes falling. The dog gave a soft bark. She took the roast beef platter from the refrigerator. After cutting the meat into small pieces, she lowered the dish to the floor. At the table she ate her breakfast. The dog finished eating and meandered around the kitchen, sniffing the floor. She rose and set their dirty dishes in the sink.

She flipped on the television for a report of the weather conditions. No improvement. She leaned down and scooped Jane into her arms. Upstairs, she set the dog on the floor and proceeded to the easel. Before grabbing a brush, her phone rang. "Hello." She paused. "Sami Lynn, how are you doing?" After several minutes of conversation, the dog barked. "I have to go. Yes, you heard a dog. She came to the backdoor last night. I plan to take her to the vet as soon as I can get off the mountain. Call me when you hear word of your promotion."

She lifted the dog. "Love ya, Sami Lynn. Bye for now."

Downstairs, she opened the door, and Jane toddled into the snow. Once the dog and Lily returned to the studio, she recommenced painting. "You might want to take a nap," she said to the dog. As if the dog knew what she said, Jane lay on the floor.

When the snow no longer fell and the icicles from the eaves began melting, she called the veterinarian's office and explained the situation. The receptionist scheduled an appointment.

On the day of the appointment, she dragged her feet and pondered. What if the dog belonged to a family? She hated the idea of giving up Jane. She enjoyed having the dog close. With a frown pasted on her face, she and Jane climbed into the car. Unlike some dogs, Jane appeared to enjoy the ride down the mountain. At the vet's office the veterinarian examined the dog and detected a microchip. He ascertained her physical condition was good. Further, he told her that she would receive a call when he contacted the owner. She and Jane left the office.

Several days later the phone rang, and she recognized the number, as it belonged to the veterinarian's office. "Hello, Lily Hayes speaking."

"Miss Hayes, you brought a Yorkshire terrier here last week. We have attempted to contact the dog's owner, but no one answered our calls. We investigated further and learned he died and has no relatives."

"He died! No relatives?"

"That's right."

"We surmised that the dog wandered from the owner's house at about the time of his death. We spoke to his lawyer, and he revealed that the dog's name is Phoebe. The owner didn't specify the disposition of the dog in his will. Since she has no one, you can adopt her, or she goes to a shelter."

"That's not necessary. I'd be honored to adopt Phoebe."

When the conversation ended, she took Phoebe in her arms and hugged her. "You're mine now. You need me, and I need you." She laughed, and the dog licked her chin.

That night, Lily retired to bed and thanked God for sending Phoebe to her to lessen the loneliness and to bring joy.

COVERED IN WHITE

Victoria Fletcher

Mary Ellen swung the ax high above her head. One last strike would get enough wood to last a month. She felt like she needed it because the Farmer's Almanac had predicted a big snow just after Thanksgiving. She had to take care of her children now that her husband, Mike, had died in a mining accident. Without Mike's income, and with only the supplement she got from the mine, it was hard to have enough. She did laundry for people and sold baked goods to the store to make ends meet. They didn't have much, but they were a happy family. Mikey was now in sixth grade and was able to help with the other chores around the house. She always tried to do the chopping of wood, though, since he hadn't learned how to use an ax yet. Katie Ann was a third grader and did well in school. Mary Ellen hoped she would have a bright future. Little Emmy Sue was just five years old and had just started kindergarten. She enjoyed school too.

Mary Ellen thought, *At least my girls have a chance at a bright future. I'm worried that Mikey wants to follow in his daddy's footsteps and work in the mines. I pray he won't. My daddy lost his leg in a roof collapse. He couldn't work, and it was a real burden on my momma and him. My daddy only lived a few years after that. My momma said she thought he died of sadness, since he couldn't work to support his family. I sometimes wondered why I married Mike while knowing he was a miner—but I loved that man.*

"I've got to carry this wood to the porch and stack it," Mary Ellen said aloud in order to break the thoughts about the mines that were going through her head.

After several trips the wood was neatly stacked on the porch, right beside the door. *That should be enough for the snowstorm,* thought Mary Ellen.

The sound of the school bus interrupted her thoughts. Soon the sound of laughter and her children chattering away rang through the hills around them.

"How was your day?" asked Mary Ellen.

"Mama, it was so good. My teacher asked me to read my poem for the assembly next week. Will you help me practice," asked Katie Ann.

"I sure will. I am so proud of you, honey," said Mary Ellen. "And how about you, Emmy Sue?"

"It was good. We get to go to the petting zoo next week if you sign my form. Oh, and we have to pack our lunch. Can you do that for me, Mama?" asked Emmy Sue, her brown eyes wide.

"I will sign your form, and I can pack you a lunch for that day," said Mary Ellen. Then, turning to Mikey, she asked, "Well, son, how was your day?"

"Like usual, I guess. Except we had a guest speaker. He was a recruiter for the Air Force. He was interesting. I brought some brochures home to look at and talk to you about. He is coming back next week to see if anyone is interested in going into the Air Force when we graduate."

"Isn't it a little soon to be thinking about graduation?" asked Mary Ellen.

"I thought so too. But Colonel Davis said he would like to see us placed in the program that goes all through high school. It prepares you and sees if you are a good match. I think I might like to try it, but we'll talk more about it. I want to do what makes you happy and what would help the family the most," said Mikey.

"I remember how you loved to see the planes at the airport when your daddy would take us there on his day off," said Mary Ellen.

"I did. I loved to hear daddy's stories about all the faraway places he would like to see someday. I thought I could see them for him since he's gone," said Mikey, a sad tone in his voice.

"You are becoming a fine young man, son," said Mary Ellen, tears streaming down her cheeks.

"What's wrong, Mama?" asked Emmy Sue.

"Nothing, honey. These are tears of pure joy and pride for my three kids," said Mary Ellen.

The kids all gave their mama a big hug.

"We need to go to the store and get some supplies in case we get the snowstorm they are expecting. How about we stop at the diner to get a burger and then go pick up what we need?" asked Mary Ellen.

The kids were all talking at once and were excited to get burgers. That had been a luxury since their daddy had died. Money was scarce.

After picking up their supplies and getting them put away, Mary Ellen told the kids to go get their homework done before bath time. Emmy Sue didn't have any homework, so she went right to her bath. Mikey and Katie Ann finished their homework and baths. They played a few hands of Crazy Eights before time for bed. They all slept peacefully.

When they awoke, everything was covered in white. Four feet of snow had fallen during the night.

The kids were excited to have a snow day. Mary Ellen asked Mikey to help carry in some wood to keep the fire going. Then she fixed breakfast for them. They usually had oatmeal or cereal, but since they didn't have to rush to get ready for the school bus, she scrambled some eggs, made biscuits and gravy, and added a piece of country fried ham.

"Burgers last night, and this fine breakfast this morning. Umm-umm. Makes me feel like a rich man," said Mikey.

The others laughed but agreed with him.

The snow days just kept coming. They had put together two one-thousand piece puzzles, played numerous hands of Crazy Eights, played a couple of I Spy games, colored and drew, read books they had been wanting to read but couldn't because of their schoolwork, and listened to the radio. But they were starting to get bored and wanted to get back to see their friends at school.

It was eighteen days later before the snow began to melt. Mary Ellen wrapped them up good and let them go out to make a snowman and do snow angels before all the snow was gone. They had lots of fun making snow angels. It was even more fun to make their snowman. Mary Ellen had brought their daddy's mining hat to put on the snowman. Mikey used the pipe his mama had given him as a keepsake after his daddy died. The girls used raisins and a carrot to make his eyes, nose, and mouth. It was a fine looking snowman. Mary Ellen enjoyed the time with her kids. *They are growing up so fast. I know I won't always have them close by me like I do now. But I am hoping they can make good lives for themselves and for families of their own. They sure are good young'uns.*

Snow days were not so much fun anymore because they knew they would be going on summer vacation now. They got to return the week before Christmas and enjoyed that time with their friends.

Katie Ann read her poem during the assembly, and Emmy Sue got to go to the petting zoo with her class. She was so proud to get to carry her daddy's work pail with her lunch in it. Mikey talked with Colonel Davis and decided he would like to try the Air Force program in high school.

"Mama, I would like to go into the Air Force Cadet program if you agree. Colonel Davis told us we would have all of our class needs paid for through the program in high school. Then, when we pass the class and go into the Air Force, we would be paid each month, just like working a job. After the six month trial period, we would be placed in the area we were best suited for and would be paid each month for the four years we were there. And if we like it, we can stay longer. What do you think? I could send money to help you while I'm gone. And we get to come home for visits three times a year for three days at a time, and once for a week. How about it, Mama?" Mikey said, almost in one breath.

"Son, if it is something you would like to try, then I say to go for it!" Mary Ellen was glad he had chosen something other than the mines.

"Thank you, Mama. I want to help the family, and I think I can while also doing something I enjoy," said Mikey.

"Sounds wonderful to me," said Mary Ellen.

This family grew up poor but didn't know it. What was lacking in money was made up for in love—love for their mama, their home, and each other. I believe they were richer than most.

About the Authors

JAN HOWERY
"A Birthday Party"

Jan Howery, a native of Southwest Virginia, writes with an Appalachian influence. Her many writings include a short story, "The Daisy Flower Garden," featured in the book *Broken Petals*. Other writings include fashion and health columns for the magazines, *Voice Magazine for Women* and *Modern Day Appalachian Woman*.

BETTY KOSSICK
"Appalachian Christmas Eve Storm"

Betty Kossick is a freelance magazine journalist, with interviewing as her forte. Over her career, her varied writing covers a broad range from newspaper press releases, news stories, columns, and features. She's been honored to interview world fame notables. In addition, devotionals and poetry continue to appear in both the religious and secular press. She's been honored with awards and recognitions for both her writing and community service: The Distinguished Service Carroll Award, Listen America Eagle Award, Celebrate Women, Woman of Worth, and The Star in A Galaxy of Verse, among others. She's the author of *Beyond the Locked Door* (2006), and *Heart Ballads* (2009). *The Manor* is her third solo book.

CHERYL LIVINGSTON
"The Best Gift"
"Evening in Paris"

Cheryl Livingston lives in the mountains of East Tennessee, where she and her husband cut, push, and prod pieces of colored glass into creations of stained-glass art. She also enjoys reading *The Crayon (W)Rapper*, a children's book which she wrote and illustrated, to schools and art classes.

LINDA HUDSON HOAGLAND
"The Naked Christmas Tree"
"An Un-Merry Day"

Linda Hudson Hoagland is the author of fiction, nonfiction, short stories, poetry, and stage plays. Hoagland has won numerous awards for her work, including first place for the Pearl S. Buck Award for Social Change and the Sherwood Anderson Short Story Contest. Her work has appeared in many anthologies and literary magazines.

LORI C. BYINGTON
"New Member of the Family"

Lori C. Byington lives in Bristol, TN with her husband, their son, and two dogs. She is an Assistant Professor of English at King University in Bristol, and she loves to write, teach, and cook/bake. Lori also snow skis during the winter; her son is on the Beech Mountain Academy Ski Team at Beech Mountain, NC. Lori has a Quarter Horse, Warrior, who is her therapy and her exercise.

PRISCILLA ARNOLD
"Changes"

Priscilla Arnold is a long-time reader, preferring the romance and mystery genres. One day she was struck by an idea and punched the keys on her computer. Thus, she created a short story which led to many more fictitious tales. She resides in Bristol, Tennessee.

VICTORIA FLETCHER
"Covered in White"

Victoria Fletcher was a former teacher and secretary/ministry assistant at First Baptist Church in Damascus, Virginia. She retired in 2018 to pursue her publishing business, Hoot Books Publishing, which is located at the Virginia Highlands Small Business Incubator in Abingdon, VA. Currently, she has written 21 books.

**Jan-Carol
Publishing, Inc**

"every story needs a book"

WWW.JANCAROLPUBLISHING.COM

www.ingramcontent.com/pod-product-compliance
Lightning Source LLC
Chambersburg PA
CBHW031902170626
46807CB00004B/1850